to one Diane from another!
Happy 50th!

Emma Thomson's
Felicity Wishes

Viking

Published by the Penguin Group

Penguin Putnam Books for Young Readers, 345 Hudson Street,
New York, New York 10014, U.S.A.

Penguin Books Ltd, Registered Offices: Harmondsworth, Middlesex, England

First published in Great Britain in 2001 by Hodder Children's Books, a division of
Hodder Headline Limited.
First published in the U.S.A. in 2002 by Viking, a division of Penguin Putnam
Books for Young Readers.

10 9 8 7 6 5 4 3 2 1

Written by Emma Thomson and Helen Bailey
Illustrated by Emma Thomson
Felicity Wishes © Emma Thomson, 2000
Licensed by White Lion Publishing

Felicity Wishes: Little book of Happiness © Emma Thomson, 2001

ISBN: 0-670-03591-2
Printed in China

Emma Thomson's

felicity Wishes

me and you

tea for two

Little book of Happiness

with love
♡

Viking

Happiness is when
someone makes you feel
really special!

Just like a fairy princess.

Happiness is
waking up on. . .

Christmas morning!

I wonder what this could be?

Happiness is

relaxing. . .

In a bath full of

bubbles!

Don't let the water get cold!

Happiness is. . .

A full box
of chocolates!

Strawberry cream's my favorite!
Maple is

Happiness is
having friends to share. . .

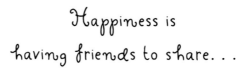

strawberry cake

chocolate cake

chocolate brownies

lime jello

shortbread

oops!
not
on
the
diet!
haha!

Lots of yummy things!

Happiness is finishing your
homework...

house work...

On time!
(so you can read)

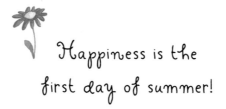

Happiness is the
first day of summer!

and having a summer
                    birthday!

Is there any honey today?

Happiness is when
you feel. . .

As beautiful as a butterfly.

And your feet don't touch the ground!

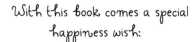

With this book comes a special
happiness wish:

Hold the book in your hands and
close your eyes tight.
Count backwards from ten and
when you reach number one whisper
your wish . . .
. . . but make sure no one can hear.
Keep this book in a safe place and,
maybe, one day your wish will come true.

Love *felicity*

oh, and feel free to wish
again any old time!